Copyright © 2025 by Trinity Publishing Company

All rights reserved. No part of this book may be reproduced or transmitted in any form or by any means, electronic or mechanical, including photocopying, recording, or by any information storage and retrieval system, without permission in writing from the author, except for the inclusion of brief quotations in a review.

Published in USA by Trinity Publishing Company

Paperback ISBN: 978-1-964707-66-2

Book Cover and Illustrations: Saba Mouri

Client Relations Specialist: McKoy Moss

It's morning time, so
I stretch my arms up.
I can feel the warmth of the sun.
My name is Dre, and it's a good day.
I can't wait to have some fun!

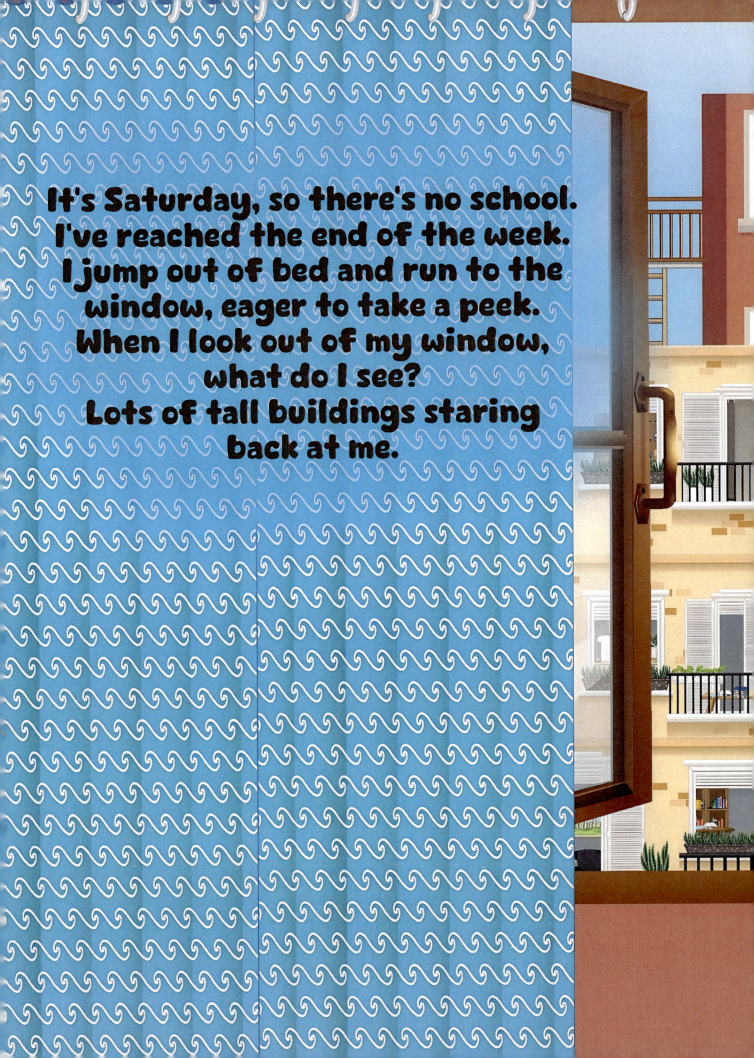

It's Saturday, so there's no school.
I've reached the end of the week.
I jump out of bed and run to the window, eager to take a peek.
When I look out of my window, what do I see?
Lots of tall buildings staring back at me.

Cars whizzing by, buses, and bikes too!
And so many people with lots of things to do.
I'm a city kid.
It's where I live.
I think that it's all good.
I love who I am.
I love where I'm from.
I love my neighborhood!

I run to the bathroom
and brush my teeth.
I also wash my face.
I go to the kitchen to eat my breakfast,
but first I say my grace.
I'm grateful for the eggs and juice.
I am grateful for the toast.
I'm grateful for my mommy.
She is who I love the most.

"Go get dressed," my mommy says, "so we can go outside."
And soon we're walking out of the door to catch the elevator ride.

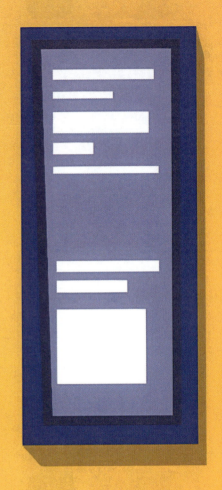

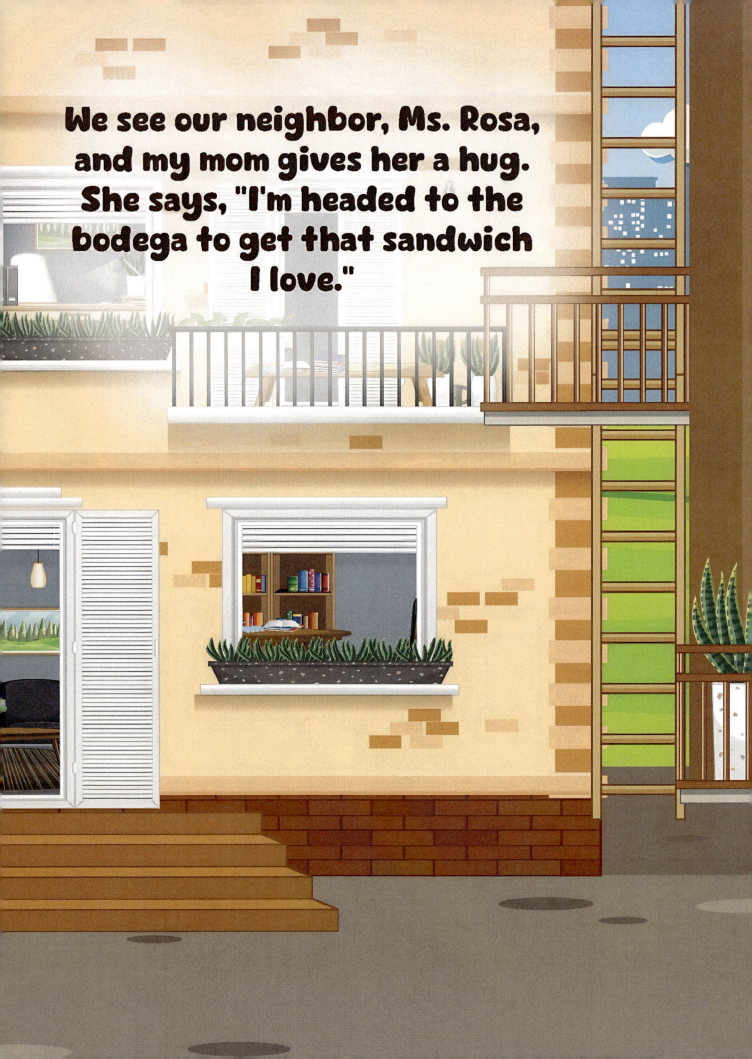

We wave goodbye and keep on moving, heading up the street.
A car goes fast right beside us, playing a booming beat.
I know that song, I like it too.
I start to clap my hands.
My mommy smiles and snaps her fingers, doing a little dance.

I'm a city kid. It's where I live.
I think that it's all good.
I love who I am.
I love where I'm from.
I love my neighborhood!
I know where Mommy is taking me.
I can see it up the block.
The park is there—my favorite place—but first we make a stop.

The ice cream truck is right out front, and there's a long, long line.
I wait my turn to choose a treat, I'm excited to get mine!

I see my friends as I walk inside.
They are on the swings.
They are on the slide.
They are climbing, and they are jumping.
When they see me, they come running.
Dre is here! They all say, so
I join them and start to play.

After a while, it's time to leave, but that was so much fun.
I scream, "See y'all tomorrow," because for now my time is done.
My mommy gives me a kiss on the cheek and says, come on, let's go.
I hug her tight, grab her hand, and say, "Yeah, mommy, I know."

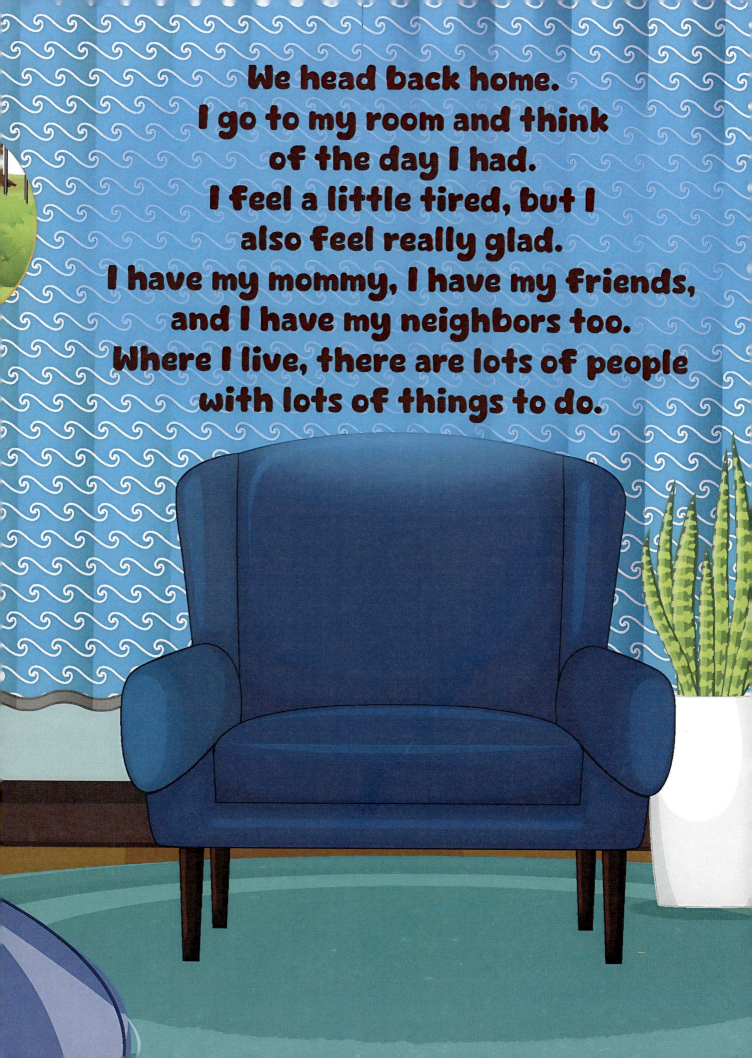

We head back home.
I go to my room and think
of the day I had.
I feel a little tired, but I
also feel really glad.
I have my mommy, I have my friends,
and I have my neighbors too.
Where I live, there are lots of people
with lots of things to do.

A Peek Inside

I Love My Neighborhood is a heartwarming story about a young boy named Dre and the simple joys he finds in his vibrant city community. From meeting his friendly neighbor in the elevator to savoring sweet treats from the ice cream truck and playing with friends in the local park, Dre's day is filled with small but meaningful moments that bring happiness and connection. As the day ends, Dre reflects on these experiences with gratitude, declaring his love for his neighborhood. This uplifting story celebrates the beauty of community life, encouraging children to find joy in their surroundings and pride in where they come from.

Made in the USA
Middletown, DE
03 February 2025